## DATE DUE

| MAY 2 0 2004 | | | |
|---|---|---|---|
| | | | |
| | | | |
| | | | |
| | | | |
| | | | |
| | | | |
| | | | |
| | | | |
| | | | |
| | | | |
| | | | |

MEDIALOG INC
Butler, KY 41006

The Penworthy Company
Milwaukee, WI 53202

1 2 3 4 5 6 7 8 9 10

❖

First Edition

# HAROLD and the PURPLE CRAYON™

## The Giant Garden

*Adaptation by Valerie Garfield*
*Based on a teleplay by Don Gillies*
*Illustrations by Kevin Murawski*

🏭 HarperFestival®
*A Division of HarperCollinsPublishers*

Harold was tucked in bed
but he couldn't fall asleep.

He was watching a little
ladybug on his windowsill.

"What is it like to be as small
as a ladybug?" Harold wondered.

He picked up his purple crayon
and drew a path.
Then he stepped onto it.

Ladybugs live in gardens,

so Harold drew a packet of seeds.

The plants grew,

and grew, and grew.

Harold felt tiny.

He felt as tiny as a ladybug!

Harold jumped from one leaf to
the other.

Then he came to a big pond.

Harold leaped onto a lily pad.

Then he drew an oar and . . .

. . . paddled right into a frog!

The frog looked very big.

The frog looked very hungry!

Harold drew a huge gumdrop.

He threw it to the frog.

*Slurp!* The frog lapped it up!

Harold paddled away very quickly.

Harold climbed over a big leaf
and saw another ladybug!

They had a tea party.

They played hide-and-seek.

How would Harold find the

ladybug?

Harold found his ladybug friend.

Oh, no!

Harold's new friend was stuck
in a spiderweb.

Harold jumped into the web.

It was sticky!

Harold drew a pair of scissors.

*Snip, snip!*

The ladybug was free!

The ladybug was so happy
to be free that she invited Harold
to meet her family.

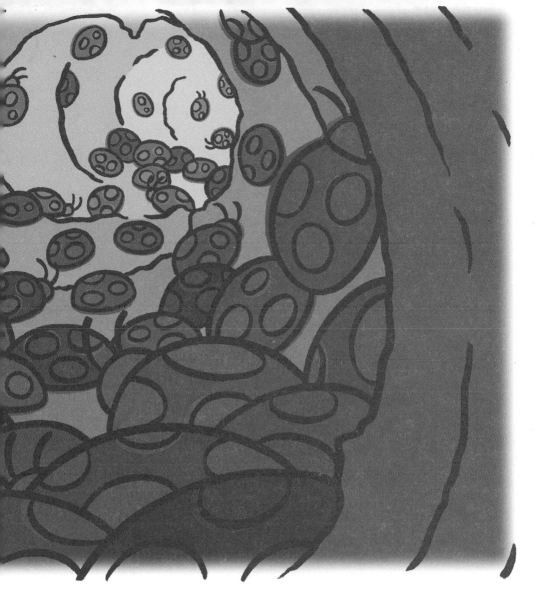

At the ladybug's home,

Harold couldn't believe his eyes.

He had never seen so many ladybugs!

He had never seen so many spots!

Harold lost his ladybug friend,

but he met an ant.

The ant was looking for food

to bring to the queen ant.

Harold helped the ant look.

They found a picnic lunch.

The ant saw some bananas

leaning against a bowl of fruit.

Harold drew a rope,

and lassoed a banana.

Harold tugged and the banana fell.

An orange rolled down onto

a plate of cookies.

It sent the cookies flying!
Harold and the ant ran
out of the way.

The cookies broke on the ground.

Harold and the ant each picked
up a piece of cookie to carry to
the queen ant.

The queen was so happy!

She made Harold her king.

Harold drew a crown and sat

beside the queen.

The queen was very nice to Harold.

She offered him some of her food.

Harold knew never to eat something

that had fallen on the floor.

Harold began to feel sleepy.

He wanted to be in his own bed.

So he set off to find the moon.

Harold found the moon.

He drew his bedroom window

around it.

He crawled into his cozy bed.

His purple crayon

dropped to the floor.

And Harold dropped off to sleep.